A NOTE ABOUT THE STORY

One evening when Warren Ludwig was reading aloud to his young daughter, he came upon an American anecdote about a hunter and a bear. On a note that came with his manuscript for *Good Morning, Granny Rose*, he wrote: "Jennifer really laughed at this one. She's four and still sucks her thumb. Now she knows that bears do too."

The anecdote has been told for generations all over America, wherever there are bears. When Warren realized that it was familiar to the people of Arkansas, it immediately appealed to him. Warren grew up there, often camping with his family in the Ozark Mountains, and he was excited about using his personal experiences in those mountains, where there are blizzards and caves, in a picture book.

In true storytelling tradition, Warren created his own characters, Granny Rose and her dog Henry, and what happens when they encounter a restless bear in the middle of winter. Warren's story and his wonderfully witty illustrations are sure to make children "really laugh at this one," just like Jennifer.

This is Warren Ludwig's first book for children, and Whitebird Books is proud to be the publisher of this talented artist and storyteller.

—*Tomie dePaola, Creative Director*
WHITEBIRD BOOKS

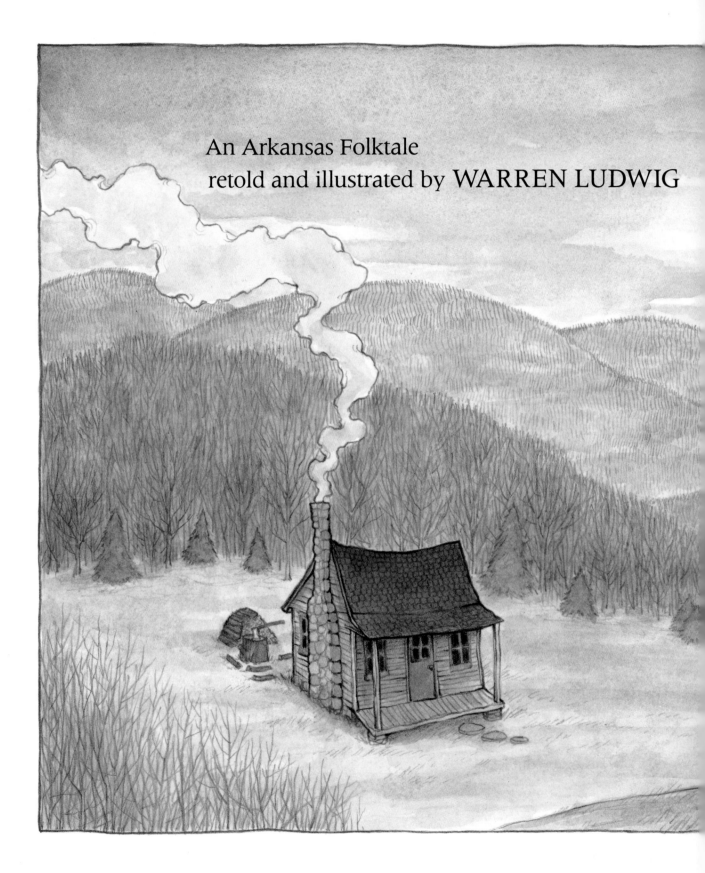

An Arkansas Folktale
retold and illustrated by WARREN LUDWIG

Good Morning,
Granny Rose

A WHITEBIRD BOOK

G.P. Putnam's Sons

New York

For Cathy and Jennifer,
with all my love

G. P. Putnam's Sons, a division of The Putnam & Grosset Group,
200 Madison Avenue, New York, NY 10016.
Published simultaneously in Canada.
Printed in Hong Kong by South China Printing Co. (1988) Ltd.
Book design by Gunta Alexander
Library of Congress Cataloging-in-Publication Data
Ludwig, Warren.
Good morning, Granny Rose/retold and illustrated by Warren Ludwig.
p. cm. "A Whitebird book." Summary: Granny Rose and her old
dog Henry get lost in a blizzard and share a cave with a sleepy bear.
[1. Folklore—United States.] I. Title. PZ8.1.L968Go 1990
398.2'1'0973—dc19 [E] 89-3753 CIP AC
ISBN 0-399-21950-1
10 9 8 7 6 5 4 3 2 1
First impression

"Don't just lay there like a sack of potatoes, Henry," Granny Rose smiled. "It's time to wake up!"

Granny Rose lived with her old dog, Henry, in the foothills of the Ozark Mountains.

Every morning she and Henry went for a walk before breakfast.

"I thought we'd head up to Lookout Ridge today," said Granny Rose. "Nothin' like watchin' the sunrise to warm ya up on a cold winter morning."

Granny Rose loved to walk in the mountains. Henry did too. Especially if he found rabbits to chase along the way.

After a while they came to the edge of a rocky cliff.
"Looks like we made it just in the nick of time," she said.

They sat down and looked out over the valley below.
"Now, Henry, you be careful," she warned. "I don't want
you wigglin' so much you fall off!"

"I reckon there ain't nothin' prettier than that,
eh Henry?" said Granny Rose. "Now let's get on home.
We've got a big day ahead of us."

As they walked back down the mountain, the wind grew much colder. Thick clouds drifted in and covered the warm morning sun.

"Looks like we might be in for some rough weather,"
said Granny Rose. Big, thick snowflakes began to fall all
around them. As the snow came down harder and harder,
Granny Rose began to worry.

"We'd better find shelter, Henry," she shouted. "I think we've walked smack-dab into a blizzard! Henry...
Henry! Where are you?"

Off in the distance Granny Rose could hear barking.
She followed the sound. "There you are! What did
you find, boy?"

"Why, it's a cave!" she exclaimed. "Good dog, Henry."

"We can rest in here 'til this thing blows over."

Granny Rose and Henry curled up together to try to
stay warm. Wet and tired, they soon drifted off to sleep.

"Grunt! Snort! Harumph!"
"Henry…was that you?" Granny Rose asked, awakened by
the noise. It wasn't Henry. It was coming from somewhere
in the cave. Somewhere close.

Granny Rose reached out into the darkness and touched
something. It was warm...and *furry*...and *big!*

IT WAS A BEAR!

"Be still," Granny Rose whispered to a very frightened Henry. "We don't want to wake him up." But as they watched the bear, he moaned and groaned. He tossed this way and that.

He rolled on his belly; then he rolled on his back.
"That poor fella's havin' a terrible time sleepin'," she said.
Granny Rose looked closer at the bear and said, "Hmmm…
just like I figured. Well, I know just the trick."

And with that, she grabbed the bear's paw and shoved it right in his mouth!

"Mmmmmmm," said the bear, and then he was quiet.
"Look at that, Henry." Granny Rose chuckled. "He's sleepin' like
a baby! I guess what my daddy always used to tell me was true."

"Bears really *do* suck their paws during their long winter nap. His must've fallen out of his mouth and he was just too sleepy to put it back in."

Granny Rose looked outside and saw that the snowstorm was over. "Looks like it's time for us to be on our way. Thanks for the use of your home, Mr. Bear. Sleep tight!" she said, and waved good-bye.

"Well, now, Henry," said Granny Rose.
"How 'bout some breakfast?"